GNEDICH

MARIA RYBAKOVA

Published with the support of the Institute
for Literary Translation, Russia

Glagoslav Publications

GNEDICH
by Maria Rybakova

Translated by **Elena Dimov**

Book created by Max Mendor

Published with the support of the Institute
for Literary Translation, Russia

© 2015, Glagoslav, Nederland

Glagoslav Publications Ltd
88-90 Hatton Garden
EC1N 8PN London
United Kingdom

www.glagoslav.com

A catalogue record for this book is available
from the British Library.

ISBN: 978-1-78437-954-4

CONTENTS

SONG I

The rage that killed so many,
the wretched rage of Achilles
who knew that he would perish,
that he would perish young,
yet he, Gnedich, will die lonely
and will probably also die young.
(It is better this way — otherwise
lonely old age—
they say it is worse,
than lonely youth,
even though then you had nothing to eat
and sat alone every evening,
and even when you did have money
and went to the brothel, women shied away
but then grew accustomed to you
because you were kind
and sad — and life was passing by, where every day
was death.)

Homer says: youth is always frightening,
and the memory of it is the most dreadful of all.
Sing, goddess, it is your amusement —
to sing our sorrows, our pain is your glory,

but when you come to me
pretending to be an actress
I will agree to suffer, said Gnedich,
and looked in the mirror with one eye.
In the dark hole of glass he saw
either the Cyclops or the hero-lover,
then Homer, then suddenly no one really,
just furniture and the sickly candle
(without even the hand that held it),
myre alge, woes unnumbered,
a thousand sorrows, much grief,
algos is pain, *algeo* — I suffer,
but in Greek even suffering is good,
and in Russian it is nothing but pain.

The pain is etched upon me
(Gnedich says)
and now everyone reads: don't come to him,
don't love him,
but take pity on him,
even though he does not need your pity.
He hurled many strong souls into the invisible world...
Who? Achilles. Let us not be distracted,
(the sound of hoofs outside the window, the piercing voice of
a tradeswoman)
into the gloom of Hades — god and place — an invisible god,
for the invisible one is dead,
dead as one who is afraid to be looked at,
one at whom they are afraid to look,
one whose reflection
even the mirror prefers to blink away as a tear

so it will not obscure the world,
perfect and everlasting.

He hurled souls to Hades and bodies
to dogs and to hungry vultures
so we would be divided after death,
as a butcher does in the marketplace:
souls there, bodies here
(and both are gloomy),
my face was beautiful, Gnedich says,
and then became ugly,
but as for my soul —
I don't know.
I suspect it is invisible,
and probably also dead,
herein Jove's will is accomplished,
my life is counted, my death
is assigned. I did not have love.
I did not have glory. Only words
I was left with — Greek —
to bind them with the Russian ones.

He often thinks about the daughter of Chryses, unnamed.
Her father came for her and she disappeared,
following her father without a word
and would not be seen with any heroes anymore.
This virgin without a name
belongs to her father, and he belongs to Apollo,
and all of them are in the transparent sphere, where only
                              devotion exists,
only awe, only prayer.
She, having descended from the ship, dissolves

in the hands of her father
as wallpaper fades,
as walls crumble, as moisture evaporates,
without passion, without a name.
If he could also erase himself from the horizon
without pain…
But no, he is retraced, scratched out, he is cut
in the marble like the letters.
I turn to the mirror —
try to read it, but nothing is clear,
there are no chroniclers for me
(he smiles and ties his silk scarf
around his neck).

The elder walks at the edge of
the bustling sea,
polyphloisbos
where the waves accrue on the sand with a splash,
with foam, with thunder — and crawl back with a hiss;
silent, he is walking on the shore
in the never-ending noise of the abyss.
The sea does not listen to man,
but man thinks
he understands the language
in which the water talks
to him.

Every time they brought a note from her
he searched for the word "yours."
God of mice, hear my prayers,
let her fall in love with me!
(The god of mice does not answer,

but quietly scratches in the corner
and rustles the wallpaper
all night.)

The ghosts of actors wander in the theater,
the shadows of heroes wander in Troy,
the shadows of words wander in the soul.
While you are asleep, she loves you,
Homer speaks to you, both of you can see,
both are alive, and life is beautiful
(but awakening heroes are crying
and ghosts are fading away).

After the sickness passed, they still didn't allow him
to see himself in a mirror for a long time,
but he was so happy that he had recovered he didn't care
because delirium — even if you are just twelve —
takes you to places
that are too dark.
He did not remember tulips in bloom there,
nor rivers of forgetfulness flowing.
He remembered only the grey air,
as though the earth was enveloped in clouds
and no sky. When he woke up
and started to catch with one eye
the light that flowed from the window
between the flower curtains
and heard the rooster's cry and the bark
of fleetly-bounding dogs, oh, how he wanted to hug
them all!
Because over there in the gray sky-less air,
there was no one near. No chicken, nor cats

nor Avdotya, nor warm milk,
not even the cobweb, trembling,
when the window pane was open,
absolutely nothing at all: only he alone,
but how can one be that way — at twelve years old —
all alone —
and there?

Then he realized that he had become a monster.

We went to the fortuneteller, Gnedich said,
but she did not tell me anything,
rien du tout (he added
in bad French). Whatever she might try to do:
lay out the cards, or burn the wax,
or read the lines on the palm of a hand
or guess the future through birds in the sky,
or pour coffee grounds into a saucer,
or interpret dreams — nothing would come of it.
I have no future.
Je n'ai qu'un livre (I have only one book),
my childhood favorite *The Iliad*.
I read it only after the illness.
I do not want to remember what I was — before —
(but I heard I was a handsome child
who was loved by everyone; played outdoors
with the children of peasants mostly,
and ran fastest of all. And shouted louder.)

The sorrowful maiden leaves with others,
she always leaves.
The loyal friend Batyushkov used to say:

maidens will always elude.
That's why we love them,
they are like water,
but do not quench thirst,
we look into them to see our own reflections —
and love ourselves in them,
and rejoice, not knowing
that this dark and dreadful whirlpool
can draw us in.
(Poor madman, how he knew his own life,
even when everything was already lost
he used to say:
I walked, I carried a flagon on my head
full of jewels,
the flagon fell and broke,
what was within it — who can tell now!
and he turned to the wall,
where he saw mountains, valleys, rivers,
battlefields, the ruins of cities,
the faces of dead comrades,
because time became one solid wall
in his room
and the plaster on this wall was crumbling away).

Briseis was taken away because Achilles let her go.
He was silent, she was silent.
Later, Ovid would guess at her hurt,
he would say through her lips: How could you let me go?
and cry.
But Homer made it more dignified: both are speechless,
no scenes, no tears.
My hidden love, Gnedich says,

even if everybody guessed,
I would say nothing; maybe she
would fall in love with my silence —
if she did not love my voice.
(Children's fairytales: the monster was hiding, hiding,
only allowed others to hear its voice,
but only after it had fallen silent, the sweetheart fell
                                        in love with it.
Only after it perished.
If the seed doesn't die, it will remain alone,
but if it dies, others will love it —
this is what it turns out the priest was saying.
I always suspected there was some meaning in all these stories.
I remember, in Poltava,
when Father Paphnutius was very drunk,
and was crying huge tears during the service,
he was telling the whole truth,
he was like a prophet, but we were all scared.)

Have you ever seen the sea,
endless, looking like the wine's darkness,
have you spread your hands to the abyss
calling for your mother? She was rising like a mist
on the grey water (Batyushkov and Gnedich
compared their recollections. There were few of them.
They agreed on one thing: a goddess cannot live
with a mortal for a long time, she disappears
to the place where there are mermaids, and shadows,
                                        and mothers.
After death women turn into air,
Batyushkov used to say,
and men into earth. Gnedich agreed with him,

but thought, *if she suddenly falls in love with me,
maybe I'll also become air?*).

When they were young, they regretted
that their mothers did not see them,
because happiness, and glory, and women
almost fell into their hands,
and later they had to be happy
that their mothers were not there anymore
and they would not notice either derangement,
or how the person becomes
an addition to the desk
in a department office or library.
Both are servants (but thought they were poets),
two bachelors (but thought they were lovers),
two invalids — not imaginary — wandering
along a dark road to gloomy hell,
like Catullus' sparrow.
Two sparrows —
that's what they were, as it turns out!
Two ruffled birds — one crooked,
the other mad.
Birds do not go crazy,
only people
who turn into birds,
Philomela without a tongue and
Procne, who killed her son,
became a swallow and a nightingale.
During one of the visits
Gnedich leaned over to his friend,
and the other whispered a secret to him:
to lose one's mind is to become a bird,

and nodded at the window: do you hear their voices
in the tree tops? They are speaking Greek.
Gnedich had to agree,
so as not to disturb the sufferer.
Then he walked home.
The sun was already setting.
The gods must have partied all day,
Apollo played on the lyre for them
and the muses sang a round.
Then they went to the chambers
built for them by Hephaestus
and rested in the happy sleep
of immortals.

SONG II

He slept badly
in the silence of the celestial night
he woke up and thought:
why wouldn't she come into my dreams?
There were only the endless corridors,
crannies, chandeliers, lobbies,
dressing rooms, dusty curtains, decorations,
an empty hall and somewhere from the street – the sound
                                        of applause.
And in his dream he understood that it must be the other way
around,
that everything had changed places, but he did not stop,
searching for her between the velvet chairs,
artificial mountains, houses and trees,
silent violins and contrabasses,
he even forgot who he was actually looking for,
and only when he woke up in despair
that he had not found her,

he remembered: Semyonova. He, ugly as hell,
was in love
with a diva and gave her lessons in stage speech.

He lights a candle,
so as not to think about the impossible
and not to lure him into sin,
which would be a shame even to confess.
Wouldn't it be better to eat something,
a piece of bread with lard,
drink some cold tea,
and work some more on the translation,
while the city is so quiet
in the silence of the celestial night.
When he came here for the first time,
he wrote to his sister: What a terrible city
at night! Silence, as in the grave.
Not like in Poltava where nights are sonorous,
roosters cry, dogs howl,
even the cattle wake up and moo,
and if everything becomes silent,
crickets begin to chirp like mad, –
all in all a regular night, but here...
Then he became used to it, he liked waking up
before everyone and thinking about the sleeping ones
in this silent city –
about Finns and Germans with their inexplicable dreams,
about the palace where the Emperor slumbered,
about the yardmen, who perhaps even in their dreams
                                        were sweeping,
yet he alone was awake.

There is always a pile of clean sheets of paper on the desk.
Clean as his face was before the illness,
but he covers the sheets with letters
as the disease covered his face with its horrible marks.

The ink blackens sheet after sheet,
for *The Iliad* is too long,
and there is no end in sight.
But if he stops, what will remain of him?
Neither faith, nor love, nor hope.
However, he learned the rules of ancient Greek grammar,
cases, times, endings,
aspirations ("Oh, it's not at all what you think!" –
he says to the ladies, if they feel like
listening to him in the lounge
about his work. One was telling him:
"I would never have enough patience!"
He caught himself thinking,
when her beauty passes,
that patience would be her fate, but immediately
forced himself to quote
a particularly striking verse,
because in his childhood a doctor told him:
"Always admire others,
do forget about yourself: cripples are malicious," –
and the boy swore: "I will love,
so be it hopelessly, but – always!
as others love."
Naïvely, he believed,
that a man's life passes in love and war,
not in re-writing circular letters
and abiding by the rules of etiquette).

He told Batyushkov about the omens:
A dragon , *daphoinos* that is
both multi-colored and bloody,
crawls out from under the roots and devours infant birds,

one by one, and then at last – the mother bird,
"nor long survived he: to marble he turned," as Homer said.
Batyushkov responded: "How could this garbage
be taken as an omen of the gods? Brrr... Just imagine:
all these generals stood and watched
as a snake ate birds. I would have vomited,
and you know I'm not sensitive,
I've been through three wars." (Dear friend,
he courageously believed, that he, a soldier,
would soldier on, keep fighting,
and then his thought could not hold up anymore,
it broke into thousands of pieces,
where verbs were by themselves,
and nouns separate,
and he remembered that the roof of a house
had the legs of a hussar,
and the door was near a little girl's mouth.)
Gnedich smiled and did not tell him,
how in the village Mikolka led him into the woods
to search for frogs,
when they, as he said, were goin' 'bout marriage
Mikolka threw them into an ant hill
and after several days he found
little bones.
He showed them to Gnedich
telling him: Do you see this hook?
I will attach it to a girl's skirt,
and the wench will fancy me.
Does it always help? – Gnedich asked.
Always, – Mikolka used to reply, and truly,
all the girls loved him. But Gnedich was never able
to throw the frog in love

for the ants to eat,
because frogs and toads were
slippery and covered in warts.

Of course, he wanted
the girls to love him,
but they smelled of sweat, and they cackled,
showing their blackened teeth,
and Gnedich decided to wait
until Moscow or Petersburg,
where the goddesses would walk
in beautiful dresses: they would be the ones to love him,
but later it appeared they also were afraid
to look at him
and Gnedich decided to wait a little more –
till his death.

Batyushkov used to say: only we follow them
down to hell.
But Laodamia? Didn't she follow
the shadow of Protesilaus
into the fire? (thus the gods tricked her) –
Gnedich objected;
but he never loved
Latin poetry
with its sensuality and appeals to drink wine,
no matter what happened, and to
throw oneself into the arms of a lustful matron
with an island alias.
He explained to Batyushkov,
that he preferred Homer:
heroes going to their deaths

and the gods' sons,
going to their deaths.
Imagine that your horses
know that you will perish
and they are crying because *they* are immortal,
and the gods are weeping,
because their children are dying,
and they can't do anything,
since Fate is harder than their will.

Batyushkov laughed and turned away,
adjusted his cuffs, put his finger to his lips,
as if to say that it's not necessary to talk about these things
and not everyone is supposed to know about them.
So you'll be translating Homer?
Yes, Gnedich answers, and slightly bows his head.
It's long time, a whole life!
Yes, Gnedich replies. Rain pounds on the window,
and life seems so short,
that it's a shame to give it up – but he decided:
to give it up to Homer...
(If he could,
he would have thrown it at the feet of a woman,
even a fallen one, because he is not looking for immortality –
but only: to give himself away, everything, every drop
of his useless life, every pore
of his face, disfigured by disease,
every muscle of his still youthful body, –
to give it away, because he remembers:
the seed, falling to the ground, must die,
otherwise it would be fruitless;
it is the only thing that he understood –

his whole self, without reserve, to give away
to the soil which would only
agree to accept him).

When he could not fall asleep, he remembered,
how he studied the Greek alphabet –
letters, which looked like loops and hooklets.
(Batyushkov told him he read in a book by some Swede
that angels in the other world write in hooks.
Gnedich laughed: but it is Greek!
Perhaps you are right, his friend agreed,
but I always thought that in Heaven
they speak Latin –
in the language of immortality and power,
but not Greek – the rustling one,
like dry leaves when the wind tears them
and carries them to the back streets, fluttering,
like our mortal souls.
Batyushkov used to write: let us rejoice.
But he in fact was longing for immortality,
and eternity; and there were rumors
that it caused his illness).

Greek letters have almost no corners
they are intertwined, and writing them
is a pleasure:
Alpha, beta and gamma, delta, epsilon, zeta, eta,
theta and iota, kappa, lambda,
mu, nu, xi, omicron, pi,
rho, sigma, tau and upsilon,
phi, like a lady's exclamation,
chi, like an official's chuckle,

psi, the strangest of letters,
and omega, the last one, which contains it all, –

but he still cannot fall asleep,
and in his mind goes through the names
                                    of the heroines of the Iliad:
Agadame, Agaue (the Nereid, it seems),
Aglaea, Aegialeia,
Aitha (no, Aitha must be a horse),
Alcyona – no, perhaps she's a seagull,
Althea and Amatheia,
Amphinome and Andromache,
Astioche, Astiochea
Briseis, Galatea, Glauce,
Dynamene, Doride, Doto,
Ianeira, Iphianassa
Iphis – and all of them
have Semyonova's face.
He knows that if he allows
the dream of her body to envelop him under the covers,
he will go to sleep instantly,
like a child under a mother's lullaby, –
but he does not want to lull himself with lies,
and continues to count,
now only those whom he happened to see.

For some reason in the homeland in Little Russia
there were so many people, even in a village,
but the capital city is so big –
yet there are no people,
so that there are even doubts,
whether you really exist,

if no one shouts to you: Wait, young master,
if no one remembers
your parents who passed away.
Just outside the village there were gullies
and a forest in the ravines,
but once, there were other villages
old walls and ashes.
Once, the lads found a skull,
and every time Gnedich looked at the manor,
he also saw ruins,
and an invisible voice kept saying: all will burn down,
but he brushed it away.
In the clearing there was a small dog cemetery,
where the deceased lady of the manor buried her pets
with French names, and where the old woman
from the last house in the village came to shepherd a goat.
The old woman had blue eyes,
which had somehow not faded with the years,
even though she complained all the time, that her husband died,
and her son was a drunk,
she threw her thick gray hair over her shoulders.
When Gnedich was nine years old, the son of the bell-ringer,
who was of the same age,
jumped down from the tower,
because his father beat him
or maybe demons tormented him during the nights,
for if they stick to someone,
they will be with him all the time.
Gnedich hardly remembered him,
that boy with the big head,
too heavy for the skinny body.
But year after year Gnedich argued with him,

as though defending his decision
not to climb those same stairs
to the same height and rush down.
He said: Now look, I was accepted to the seminary,
I study languages
spoken by ancient people,
isn't that interesting?
I was seriously ill but I survived,
and also, when the guys and I were caroling,
people gave us a lot of sweets and a whole goose,
and on top of that, you see, I started to write verses.
Later he used to say: now I am going to Moscow,
to the University Boarding School,
then to Petersburg; look
what kind of position I have:
I am invited to the salons where we talk
about fine arts,
and young ladies play the piano,
and men discuss politics,
we smoke cigars,
we know everything that is happening in Paris,
everything that is happening in London,
soon I will be introduced
to His Majesty the Emperor,
he regards favorably my translation,
and it is not out of the question that I might
even have a family of my own one day,
although it is still too early to think about that,
and he adds: look at the dazzling sunrise –
the red sky over stone Petersburg,
the rippling Neva, like the folds of a garment,
the water, so to say, *reflects the color of the sky.*

If you could only feel,
the transparency of the air,
and even this window
through which I look at the street,
is beautiful just because of its mere existence,
(unlike you, the ethereal one).

But in the depths of his soul,
especially during the night,
Gnedich is afraid,
that when his hour comes
and the bell-ringer's son, still a nine-year old,
will meet him at the threshold of the kingdom of Hades,
where he has been residing for a long time,
and will ask: So, was it worth it?
with mockery in his voice
or indeed with curiosity,
Gnedich will have nothing to say,
but will cover his face with his hands
and cry
transparent tears
from his left eye.

SONG III

Cranes were crying out and jumping in front of each other –
this was the last thing he remembered before falling asleep;
but even in his sleep cranes appeared and with a cry
fell from heaven to earth, and he covered his face with his hands,
to hide it from their sharp beaks.
Their piercing cry rang out louder and louder.
He awoke and realized that somebody was knocking at the door.
The cook said a new maid would come to clean,
he said: I'll show her myself what to do,
I don't want her to wreak havoc on my papers,
but she'd better clean off the dust.
The cook said: she will come.
He dresses in a robe and ties a silk scarf around his neck.

Maid, cook, friend, high court lady, loneliness,
if he dresses impeccably, clothes himself in armor –
under the cover of French fashion he fears no one.

He opens the door and sees a pale creature
of indeterminate age, who lifts her eyes at him –
almost white (*is she Finnish?*)
but quickly lowers them (*he looks like a devil!*)
and says that she is Elena, that the cook sent 'er in,

that she's sorry fer bein' late,
but the rope was wet and she couldn't untie the boat
'er brother olways binds 'em knots so's you can't untie 'em;
she told 'im the other day that she was goin' t' see a gentleman,
there was no way she could without the boat,

                                                      they live on an island,
this is why she was late; she swears no one in town
cleans better.

He nods and makes a sign with his fingers.
She pauses, enters, he shows her to his study –
the desk he writes on, a pile of books,
a cabinet and another cabinet with a dusty smell,
an ottoman, and an armchair, and a little table,
where his pipe lies,
and in an adjacent room, the narrow bed of a bachelor,
an icon in the corner
of the Mother of God with everlasting light in front of her,
and the pale creature nods and is no longer afraid,
because if this devil keeps in his office
any devices of sorcery,
the Virgin Mary will look after her since her image is not in vain.
The featherbed is made with fine and costly linen
(*she manages to notice*); but it isn't shaken up;
and the windows are so large, but dim – they should be washed,
the light barely passes through 'em;
he sure burns many candles, expensive, wax,
even in the daytime. These gentry are often up at night,
God knows why: one sits and sits alone by 'isself
casts a spell – who can understand 'em:
there may be icons at their home,
as though everything were normal,

but why are the rooms so huge if
they are so empty – a chair there, an ottoman here,
a desk in the corner – so much space is filled with nuffink.
He'd better get some trunk
or a cupboard with carved doors,
and the ceiling is so high
as if a devil is flying beneath it.
(She imagines it and smiles, but then
wipes the smile from her lips so he won't think
she's laughing at him.)

He says: You'll come at noon,
because that is when I leave for my office
at the Imperial Public Library.
The words are so heavy that she kneels and bows,
when he speaks them.
I don't want even a speck of dust in the room,
nor any cobwebs in the corners – she nods –
and the books should remain in the same place

and on the same page, and the papers should not be out of order.
She nods, and he strives in vain to catch sight of
any thought on this pale face.
Well, she probably understood. Elena,
what a name for a poor maid,
but, it may be a sign that
the gods are pleased with his work of translation!

He says goodbye to her, leaves the house,
walks along the waterfront,
looks at the fishermen – one is playing a flute,
another says to him: stop it; you'll scare away all the fish,

the palaces gaze into the water, and it seems to Gnedich
that somebody is about to walk out of their front doors,
where silent lions sit turned to marble,
and call the fishermen to play the flute
to entertain the sad boyars –
but he knows there are no fairytales;
or, in any case,
where he appears – the fairytales disappear.

In the library a letter from Batyushkov is waiting for him.
He begins to read it prior to taking up the volumes.
(From one dusty book to another dusty book –
this is his path, and he himself is ash,
and dust, and an empty word).
Batyushkov writes: "What a pity you have never been to Paris.
A maze of small streets – you'd love them!
everything is measured for man in this city.
The Cathedral is great! – like a dark forest –
and stands on spidery legs.
I have been in the palace, even paid a visit to the academy.
A pity that I did not see Parny – you know,
he is my favorite.
Remember, you said once that you had dreamed a city
where everything was ugly: houses, clothes, songs,
chariots, the river, commoners, streets –
everything had sharp angles and everything was like
a wasteland, although you could still find people there.
You told me about this over a cup of coffee,
without fear of ridicule
(since only old hags
confide to each other their dreams and guess at their meaning),
you kept saying: what if such a city exists or would exist?

I have to admit that you scared me. I thought for a long time
about such a possibility and came to the conclusion
that maybe, for a minute, you had a glimpse of hell,
and that in hell our souls will be tormented by ugliness,
because the soul is not devoid of eyes,
but hell is devoid of beauty;
as for the realm of men,
I swear by our friendship, my friend Gnedko,
people will never build houses
like the ones you dreamed,
looking like boxes
which had their wrapping paper ripped off;
the soul requires beauty, it feels beauty,
the soul longs for it in the earthly vale,
it recalls what it had seen in Heaven,
as Plato teaches us,
therefore it compels hands
to raise palaces and temples,
and even in the poorest hut
to paint the window casing in azure.
That's why we love beauties and read Homer,
and listen to the violin; however, consider yourself
beloved of the gods, for it is they who let
you, my friend Gnedko, look straight into hell –
probably so that you would
translate more Greek poetry for us!
Menin aide thea peleiadeo Achileos.
So many vowels point, no doubt,
to the divine origin of the Greek language.
But I have been distracted; this is what I wanted to tell you:
get a passport for yourself and come here.
I'll show you Paris and I'll show you Germany.

If we are lucky,
we may even see Goethe.
You need to travel in the world while still young ,
you have buried yourself in papers, and never show your head.
Carpe diem, as Horace says,
life passes and youth does not return."

The letter continued for two more pages.
Gnedich put it aside and opened his Homer,
but the reading was not going well, he looked out the window
through the thick glass at the city,
not the morning city but the dim one under the northern sky;
he thought: maybe I ought to go see it all,
but he knew he would not, and a tear rolled down
onto the translation and smeared the ink.
Someone saw a dragon, was startled and stopped,
in the wooded canyon in the mountains of Hellas;
his knees trembled, and he turned and ran.
Paleness spread across his cheeks: but then he himself had never
seen a dragon in the wooded ravines of his childhood.
Snakes, sometimes frogs, even lizards,
but a dragon – there was no such thing,
although he often imagined how, maybe,
a dragon was lurking in the ravine and guarding a princess,
and he, Gnedich, would go and free her, and slay the dragon.
To live and to win, one needs to get rid
of pity for the vanquished
of self-pity – but how, how
to conquer oneself?
How to see himself as nothingness,
how not to regret the fleeting days,
how to tell yourself: you're just one of many,

your job is to translate Homer,
to be loved – is not your business,
being a hero is a job for others,
and immortality belongs to the gods,
so do not pity a body, whose every part
advances toward the grave, don't pity a face
lost to disease.
Well, he agrees, he does not feel sorry for himself,
but how not to grieve for his sister –
he was not there when she was dying,
he would never forgive himself... Oh, why does life
consist only of missed farewells,
anything that might happen to me is
too small a punishment
for the blackness of my soul, hidden from all,
but known to me;
when I cannot sleep at night,
the darkness of the Lord seems so transparent,
but the blackness in my soul pours out
like spilled ink,
flooding the entire bedroom, sticks eyelashes together
and I can see neither the darkness of the Lord, nor His light.

And Elena, if it's after midnight and she is not yet asleep,
listens to mice rustling in the hall,
a lonely bird suddenly cries out in the night,
and then all falls silent – fall asleep, asleep,
into a deep and dark sleep without dreams,
like water in the well,
like the earth on a moonless night.
A little ray of light will wake you at daybreak.
It opens the flowers that had closed themselves for the night,

it stirs the feathers of the sleeping ruffled birds,
listen, birds: it's time for you to spread your wings.

At sunrise, Elena goes out,
walks barefoot in the dew,
washes up and raises her face to the sun,
her brother has not yet awoken,
and her brother's wife sleeps for a long time,
but Elena has already untied the boat
and is gliding along the river.
At noon she enters his house
with a basket and rag.
Yard keepers and cooks in this city talk about her –
no other woman cleans better,
never any complaints, clean as in paradise.
She dusts the books, wipes the shelves.
Her brother knows how to read and she could learn
from the priest in the village – but why would she?
Those book covers are dark and the scripts are weird.
She wipes the inkstand, wipes the pen –
the pen the one-eyed master's fingers had picked up,
the master's palms had touched this desk.
For the first time in her life she senses
that she wipes not just dust
but his fingers' touch;
although the master is not in these rooms,
he was there in the morning and would be in the evening,
but even now there is something of his presence:
an invisible trail, unnoticeable spirit.
She goes into the bedroom and
crosses herself in front of the icon;
begins to shake up the featherbed,

straightens the sheets, fixes a pillow,
and the imprint of a lone body
preserved from the morning
disappears.

Still she has to clean those dusty windows!
Grabbing her skirt by the hemline, she climbs onto the
windowsill
with a bucket and rag, rolls up her sleeves once more
and starts to rub the glass in circles, and more circles,
wipes the sweat from her forehead, looks at the roofs
that stretch up to the Neva,
at the Admiralty Needle, at the silver water,
at the nice soft clouds;
then she starts to rub again,
and breathes on the glass,
and looks at her breath's trace
and wipes again,
so that it becomes completely crystal-clear, completely clean
in the scholarly master's apartment.

SONG IV

He left for the country in a postal carriage in the early morning.
Batyushkov had long been calling him:
Come, we'll go pick blueberries,
we'll drink wine at the table covered with a tattered tablecloth,
in the evening we'll burn candles and tell fortunes by Virgil,
it does not matter if it's already getting cold, – we'll make a fire;
after all in St. Petersburg you'll never see such red

                        and golden leaves

in the autumn,
you'll not see the abundance of berries.
and I'm bored without you, my friend.

Gnedich turned him down for a long time:
the journey was too long,
he would need to get up early, and you see he works at night,-
but in the end he went, and of course he was sick during the
journey.

When will it finally be Vologda?
He could not even think to have a bite of bread with chicken
that he brought with him in a bundle,
and at stops he preferred
to go out, breathe the fresh air on an empty stomach,

and think about how the Earth is endless,
and how flowing are her hills, which are becoming fewer
and how empty is the sky, even when it has clouds.
After a few miles it began to rain,
and continued to drizzle without becoming a downpour,
but didn't cease; then it dried up.
Along the road walked a beggar with matted black and gray hair,
a bag on his shoulders, stick in his hand.
As he passed by, Gnedich heard a song,
but could not make out the words.

"I could stop, approach him,
listen to him,
see if the song had any words,
and not just whining vowels –
Homer might have been like that –
but the vagrant was more like a drunkard
than a bard – curiosity
would not lead me to anything good;
beware, Gnedich, of sirens!"

He began to compose a jocular report
to Batyushkov on his journey
about himself as Odysseus.
At the station, while they were changing horses
he walked into a pub and asked for some tea and bread,
he took out a piece of paper, licked a pencil
"Many were the trials I met on my way," –
along the rim of cup a fly walked
stepping over and over with its thin legs,
a flare from the window glimmered on the porcelain,
too hot to touch.

And life swept over Gnedich like a dreadful wave
that he was reading for the first time and for the last,
and could only make out one word: now.
Pencil in hand, paper with grease spots
(because he put it on the dirty table),
a crack, thin as a hair, in the white cup,
the polished side of a samovar, a dark icon in the corner,
the daylight outside so dense
that you could drink, eat and cut it in pieces –
all of this happened to him, to Gnedich, just the once
and he suffocated from these things.

It was time to go back to the carriage.
He put the paper in his pocket.
The coachman whistled, the horses began
stepping with their hooves,
Gnedich started to joggle but did not try
to escape this torment in his mind,
no, he listened to his body,
as the pain throbbed in his temples,
while he allowed his heart to pulse in rhythm with its pain;
nausea rose to his throat,
yet he loved his body,
he loved his disfigured face
(that nobody else loved).

He knew that it will be taken away, like
the cup, the samovar, the pub already was,
and many miles that they passed – these miles were
                                        taken away, too,
every birch, every pine tree,
that rushed by

decreasing in size, because in the north
trees tend to be closer to the ground
under the sky's heaviness.
Birds flew lower and lower.
Gnedich sat hugging his knees,
jumping up over the potholes.
O my little life, *zoe, bios,*
how I regret that I did not love you in time:
yesterday, for example, I did not love you, as I was falling asleep,
I dreamt of Semyonova,
instead of feeling the heaviness in my legs
or watching my eyelids go down.

He took a sheet of paper out of his pocket and turned it over.
"I am Odysseus, waves rock my raft
but I landed at a welcoming island
by the name of tavern;
there I was given a foreign potion, a weak tea;
the pimpled servant did not look like a nymph;
no gardens bloomed around me, nor did birds sing;
there was, indeed, a fly –
maybe it was Athena disguised as an insect?
I did not know that and brushed her away from my cup.
It's getting late, I'll have to stay overnight somewhere,
and I only hope that at the inn
the hostess will not turn me into a beast,
but if she does –
may she turn me back human by the morning light."

The inn was so sad, as though
no one ever came here but all were merely leaving,
and even when the last ones left – nobody recalled them.

Cobwebs covered the corners and a layer of dark dust
draped everything one might touch.
Men unharnessed the horses,
the samovar happened to be cold,
the hostess really looked like a witch.
O that there would be no bedbugs in the room!
Lares clicked the floorboards,
Penates frolicked in the attic like bats.
He was falling asleep and yet could not sleep;
something was knocking at the window –
someone's heart, a homeless spirit,
a forgotten dream, my youth…
By thirty years of age we forget so many.
We'll be forgiven just because
we too would be forgotten soon.
"Batyushkov! from the hard bed,
from an inn,
from the pitch black of night
please accept my assurances of a heartfelt friendship!
I've never heard that the gods have friends –
therefore, Batyushkov, we're above the gods!"

And then in the night a bird cried broken-heartedly
to remind him of the sin of pride.

Sleep overcame Gnedich – soft, like a blanket,
the brother of death, still only a brother;
the nocturnal life of the forest that he was unaware of,
played out under the sky: snowy owls caught mice,
an eagle-owl crowed,
the sleepless paws
of beasts of prey

stepped with a soft gait.
Before dawn all was quiet;
the darkness paled, and
before the sphere of the sun rolled out,
the air vibrated.
Gnedich woke up happy, as in his childhood,
because he would soon meet his friend,
he dressed with an adult diligence,
looked at the dusty mirror,
(a crack divided his face
in half).
Refreshed, he went down the stairs,
got into his carriage, the well-rested horses
were swift, the leaves turned slightly yellow overnight,
and trees on both sides of the road
sought to embrace him.
He wondered how many tricks the world has
to keep us from going any further –
a forest canopy, a singing bird, a flower...
Take for example, Narcissus –
maybe it was not his reflection, but a ripple in the water
that forced him to gaze again and again,
the world caught him in its beauty as in a trap
and dissolved him without a trace.

Sickness again rose to his throat,
a headache from the bumps and turns.
Then the holes were over and the puddles began,
so enormous,
that they reflected the whole forest and half the sky,
wheels got stuck in the mud, they had to pull them out.
"Our land is somehow quite inconvenient,

and the body, generally speaking
has the same impassability
where our thoughts and feelings get bogged down
and all this comes to an end in a puddle,
a lump of dirt,
a handful of ashes."

But the road straightened out, and the wheels ran fast.
Trees on both sides of road flashed so quickly.
A cloud of smoke appeared in the distance,
and look: there is a manor on the horizon,
and you can already see the windows,
a triangular frontal, four columns,
now the staircase steps,
and on the steps a small figure,
that runs back and forth and waves to him.
The journey is over,
I arrived,
my friend! My friend!
rejoice.

SONG V

Batyushkov threw himself onto his neck
and shouted to the servant
to carry the guest's bag out of the carriage
while he himself continued to dance around his friend
as if performing a savage rite.
He showed Gnedich to his room
where a single oil lamp dimly burned in the hallway,
a sweet scent of the church;
they went into the hall and embraced.
Batyushkov had long ceased to notice
how constrained were the movements of his friend,
as though Gnedich felt uncomfortable
when he spread his arms and touched the other;
he stood immobile like an automaton,
raising his head high (it was not pride
but because his face was pockmarked
it should be held high),
and lightweight Batyushkov clung to him
for a few moments,
and his heart fluttered, like a bird,
dry, warm and shivering.
He took a few steps back and looked at Gnedich,
a smile flickered at the corners of his mouth,

quite boyish, and it was hard to believe
that he had gone through three military campaigns
                                and was wounded.

And, running his hand through his curls, as if in embarrassment
he pointed Gnedich to a chair –
as if to say – sit down,
light as a bird, he ran into the corridor,
to call a servant: "Vanka, Vanka,
bring us champagne!" – and added softly:
"You'll like it."
Without losing his perfunctory nobility,
Gnedich sipped the champagne and praised it,
and Batyushkov laughed from joy:
ah, how the years flee, Postumus, Postumus,
(in his youth Batyushkov was Achilles or Postumus,
and later will be: Constantine the God).
There was a glass vase on the table
with a bouquet of flowers, cut in the morning.
And the stems were reflected in the water at such
                                an unnatural angle,
that Gnedich could not break away and shift his sight
from the water to his friend's face.
And the more Batyushkov talked,
the more his eyes (from tiredness perhaps)
slid back to the water... and phrases
refracted in his mind, like these stems, in an unnatural prism,
and made Batyushkov's clear words
strange.

Batyushkov said
that he had learned how to truly hope.

He lit a candle and beckoned Gnedich
back into the hallway.
(How hard it was to break away from the shimmering water
how difficult to follow another with weary steps...)
There – carefully, so as to not to set fire to it,
he brought a candle to a spider web in a corner and showed
Gnedich
where, in the wreath of thin threads
he found hope.
Gnedich nodded,
but his pupils were too tired
to discern it.
Batyushkov expected his friend to argue,
but Gnedich struggled with sleep and only said:
yes, yes, he agreed
that hope is altogether not a thought, but an effort,
like the straining of muscles during a long run,
or when you are learning Homeric verses by heart.
The hope of a vase holds the glass around the water,
and should the vase lose hope, the glass would break,
and you'd have to call Vanka or Grishka
to sweep up and throw away the debris.
"Nowadays I hope day and night, –
says Batyushkov – But it's difficult –
and all other thoughts are interrupted."

Then they were silent: something bestial and steely
kept them in its embrace,
much stronger
than the friends' mutual touch
"I'll read you a poem" – Batyushkov says,
and Gnedich nods, though half asleep,

and words, like rivers, flow somewhere,
instead of remaining mere sounds.
The poet kisses Chloe's charms,
and who this Chloe is, he himself does not know.
Her golden hair smells like roses,
her bosom is alabaster, her steps are light.
The poet languishes, but not in earnest,
the shepherdess is about to come to a rendez-vous.
He waits for her under the fragrant shade of the trees,
whose branches are getting longer, darker and drier.
The forest, black in its madness, surrounds the poet,
with no way out at all.

But the poet keeps singing about the shepherdess,
and the ray of light about to go out,
the sorrow, the moon, the house's Lares,
the sounds of feasts, the silent walls,
and the sail devoured by the foamy abyss,
the pastures, the streams, and the dens,
and the fog and the trepidation

Then suddenly the drowsiness passed,
the fireplace blazed,
Batyushkov stared straight into the fire
as though something was alive there,
or a mistress's letters were burning.
What do you see, Gnedich wanted to ask,
instead he said: "What are you thinking about?"
For a while Batyushkov didn't respond
and it seemed to Gnedich that a cricket was singing
                                        behind the walls.
But it was not a cricket: it was silence ringing,

piercing, like an insect
(it rang, rang, and then subsided)
"About Petin," he replied
when Gnedich had already forgotten the question.
"I am thinking about Petin, a comrade of mine,
who died at Leipzig.
I walked across the field, looked at bloodied bodies
until I found him – yet two days before,
we had been talking, munching on stale bread,
washing it down with Bohemian wine.
He was restless as if something
warned him of his death, but I was cheerful as
that time in Moscow, when we were laughing all evening.
Afterwards we meant to go to the ball and have a dinner
                                        at the assembly.

We got into the carriage, but then stopped
for a moment at the Kuznetsky bridge.
we were approached by a beggar
(I am ashamed
that I only thought
how similar he looked to an engraving
I had seen in Dresden: a beggar on crutches,
without a leg, with a hungry gaze, and the hole of a toothless
mouth).
"Postumus," – Petin said, – "let's give all our money
to this poor man, and ourselves go
back home for dinner." We gave him all our banknotes.
The beggar crossed himself and plodded to a pub,
and I did not regard that we had mercy on him
but only acted justly.
Though where is this justice?
In which laws is it written that you must give everything away?

I just followed Petin.
In our unfortunate age
everyone can become a hero
without departing from the Kuznetsky bridge, without leaving
the carriage, –
but not everyone has become one though,
just Petin.

Having died so young, what did he miss?
That turn of the head at the age of thirty-something,
looking back upon the past that can produce
only one monster: experience.
Injured at Georgenburg I was lying on straw,
looked at doctors
bandaging Petin's wound,
and simply thought: he is alive, he is alive.
Even now,
if I fall on some straw
I began to hope against hope: he is alive;
but then I recall
(what is it about memory – a stone, a creek, a bluebell,
a wind in the bushes, colors of the sky
suddenly force us to believe
that the past still continues...
This world was created, my Postumus,
only to deceive us).

I saw his grave and wept over it.

I placed a simple wooden cross at its head.

I asked the priest to maintain the fence.

Petin's name will disappear,
for he has not accomplished anything
that makes people praise
or reproach somebody after their death;
for earthly immortality you need heroics,
glory or evil deeds, –
but there is yet a different kind of immortality.

(He covered his face with his hands).

The dead aren't a nothing. They are yet something, and souls
are stronger than heat
from the funereal fires,
when I sailed from England,
the sea was leaden,
the seagulls were screeching
about their love for sailors,
like brides left on the land (but were lying).
I looked for stars of the north, for the North Star,
the deck rocked and lulled us,
my eyelids closed,
and suddenly I shivered – Petin stood close by:
without wounds, or blood, or death;
he was smiling
as though I only dreamed of the funeral and the mourning,
and he had come to wake me up.
It was so good,
I wanted to shake his hand,
but only grasped at the air..."

...And Batyushkov talked about the sea calming down,
 the stars becoming brighter and the deck hardly swaying,

but his heart pounded, predicting shipwreck.
Gnedich gazed into a corner
where the darkness had completely thickened, –
and saw a silhouette of a man,
dense in his immateriality.
The man put his finger to his lips
so Gnedich would not let slip
that a third person was there in the room,
and Gnedich went to bed
rejoicing that friends do not leave us
and that he was a keeper of this secret.
He fell asleep as soon as his cheek touched the pillow,
and slept without dreams
through the rooster's crowing and cows' mooing.

In the morning all was bathed in light.
He woke up, went out onto the balcony and glanced over the
garden.
Autumn flowers raised their heads,
waiting to be cut,
the dead were sleeping in their graves,
and our Sister Death
looked at her brothers with a smile.

SONG VI

In the hallway he took
a note from the tray and opened it.
It was from Semyonova.
But why he did not recognize her name
despite seeing it many times?
It was the same handwriting:
long delicate lines, uncertain, tilted,
like a teenager's,
and on the same fine watermarked paper.
But why the name was unknown?
He always unsealed her letters with a shiver
but not this time.
The letter's magic omens
were only the Russian alphabet.
This was the name of a woman
with whom he had fallen out of love.
He had ceased loving her,
but she called him
to come in the morning to give her
another lesson in recitation.
As a seminarian,
he invented his own method of tragic speech
and became other than himself,

but the shadow of the fallen heroes in the war
or the stepmother who loved her stepson,
one of the many who've died but live
in funeral decorations of the theater
when the curtain rises between
our lives and life everlasting.
When he was becoming a god or a woman
he knew the life he was destined to live
was only a chapter
in the big thick book of opportunity.
Rising on tiptoes and turning his face to the sky
he captured the audience with his voice.
(The voice came from the chest – not from the throat –
and at the end an artery was torn
and that killed him).
The beauty
also was rising on her tiptoes
and turning her face to the skies,
and the sky looked at her face
as if at its own reflection.
He put on his thick Petersburg fur coat
and went to her house, without hiring a coachman.
Yardmen did not have time to sift through the snow
that fell during the night.
In the morning the street lamps were already lit,
their dotted line marking the length of the road,
everything was gray and cotton.
He carried
his soul like a sleepy firefly
in the unrecognizable streets.
(In the past, he knew them by heart,
every house was inundated with

the expectation of a meeting with Semyonova,
or the memory of the last meeting).
He walked and heard the shouts of the coachmen
from the world
where they cover their feet with sheepskin
that remembers the warm body of a sheep,
where they drink tea in pubs,
grasping a cup with huge fingers,
where they get married and beat their wives,
where they christen babies,
and howl over the dead,
where nobody has heard of Priam
or the marvelous city of Priam.
Gnedich wrapped himself up in the fur coat
and hurried past his own life
to give lessons of declamation
to the woman with whom he had fallen out of love.

Long ago in Kharkov
when it was a terrible cold
they ran away from school
and went to the woods
to shake the snow from the fur branches.
The heavy sound
of snow falling...
a liberated branch
soars upward,
under the tree there is
a human profile;
here! here! who is this? a peasant woman,
you can only see
a waxen face under

a layer of snow –
they run away
leaving her
in the silence of the forest,
in whiteness.

He gave his coat and hat
to the servant with flushed cheeks.
They were already waiting for him.
He went to the salon.
Semyonova was reclining on the couch;
her carefully coiffured hair
was *casually done*,
a ribbon brushing her forehead, a shawl dropping off her
shoulders;
she was like a statue
about to descend from the pedestal, but she never did.
He touched her hand with his lips and was greeted
by a half-smile.

The heart is an organ of eternity
because
even the smallest piece of it could be broken again.
He sank into a leggy chair.
Since he first saw her on the stage,
it was as if there were always two Semyonovas,
and even when love was almost killing him
they did not merge into one –
one was a goddess and the other a peasant woman
whose howling suddenly made
Polyxena's monologue
horrifying;

but now she was neither a woman nor a goddess but
someone he never met.

He said: I have an idea for a play.
She put aside a French book
and raised her eyebrows.
It began to snow outside the windows and the room went dark;
a servant came and put a brass candlestick on the table.
And the words fell like snow
on the carpet near the armchairs and fireplace;
he realized that he would never write a tragedy –
that the words were killing it but continued to talk
because Semyonova was listening:

let Hector be looking for his wife, be all of the first act
let him be wandering in the palace's labyrinths
in long hallways,
taking either a sister or maid for Andromache,
let him realize his mistake, and be searching again,
and be afraid that he will never find her
because the break between battles was short
and every battle could become the last;
and only at the very end of the first act
would he see her at the tower;
where she was standing with her back to him;
all day long
she as well
was looking for her husband on the battlefield
among the marquees and tents,
she looked and did not find him.

Snow's thick flakes tumbled down.
More candles were brought (he noticed
the servant was wearing soft slippers
and stepped soundlessly).
In the second act Andromache says:
they'll kill you and capture me
don't leave for a fight, stay with me.
But if I remain will it change fate?
Ilion will be destroyed and I will perish.
Thus I must go to battle.
Semyonova said: I don't understand,
and Gnedich hesitated not knowing how to explain
this iron necessity similar to love
which only heroes know.
And the third act?
Then he was startled
because he utterly forgot
what he had intended
to depict at the end of the play.
Everything was obliterated, covered with snow.
She looked at him with a smile,
which made her classic features less regular
(therefore, she rarely laughed).
She asked: "Would you read to me?"
and handed him a book.
Fairy tales are suitable for this time of year,
don't you think? – He reads her a fairy tale
about a beauty sleeping in the woods,
about blackthorn and dog rose,
their branches interlacing,
about a prince who was sneaking through the bushes
and saw the servants who did not have time

to empty their glasses,
saw the parrot sleeping in its cage,
and the little dog curled up beside the bed;
he himself had been that prince
when he was twelve; in the winter's
Ukrainian woods;
the pale face of a peasant woman,
her body under the snow –
he should have touched her
and she would have risen and walked.
Out of the grey the sky became a purple evening.
The servant brought some coffee in china cups,
and the conversation switched to intrigues at the theater,
then he was given his coat in the hallway
and went out into the Petersburg winter night,
which fell at four in the afternoon.
He left the fairy tale
in which all wishes come true
and entered the Greek epic where the hero
wants only one thing – to be faithful to fate.
And if death was waiting for him,
he would love his defeat.
But how beautiful were the years
when Semyonova was everything to him:
how she would put the big vase with flowers on the floor,
how she threw back her head
exposing her white throat,
and resembled a swan,
He thought:
"You could swim in my tears,
princess."

SONG VII

He wrote his thoughts down
in the small notebook
without hope that someone would read them.

The soul's breath,
the prayer,

my son's lovely soul,
your father created you
at my lips with his kiss.

Infinity is in
the forest breeze,
in the man's voice,
but since we went around the globe
it's no longer here.

Greek marble,
the poem of Simonides,
contour on a vase,
hard as the justice of ancient times
that punished the smallest of crimes
by death.

Aren't you the amber?
Saadi asked the piece of clay
No, I am simple dirt
that lived with a rose

dying like a flower
that dries without leaving a trace
of August's fragrance.

It is unlikely that to doubt immortality
means to deny God.
We are so small and the world is so big,
our claims for eternity
are clearly exaggerated.

Who put gates on the sea?
Who uttered:
Hitherto shalt though come, but no further:
and here shall thy proud waves be stayed?

In the night between the 18th and the 19th
I had a wonderful dream:
someone with the voice of Batyushkov
told me that Homer and Jesus, son of Sirach,
lived in almost the same time
and not far away from each other.
But Homer had so many words:
"hilly", "mountainous",
"powerful", "quick", "the fastest"
and the other had so many thoughts!
Homer was a chatterer
and Sirach's son was a contemplative.

Annoyed by these words
I woke up.

Gnedich wrote down dreams in the morning,
                                       thoughts in the evening.
During the day he worked at the library
where he received a salary
and had a desk near the window.
There were always new books in neat piles,
he cataloged them,
writing in his clear handwriting
the title of every volume on a note card,
he put it in a box,
an aide put the book on the proper shelf,
but Gnedich always was afraid the youth had got it wrong
so he went to check
to be sure everything was in its place.
This continued into the evening.

He forced himself not to look out the window,
not to pay attention to the people going by,
not to count the weeks and months
not to think
that he had already spent years in this hall,
that more years would come and go,
and then a few more.
Instead he wished to rejoice in
the titles of the books,
the clarity of his own handwriting,
the fact that the library
had more collections,
that it expanded like the capital

that the aisles between shelves
were similar to streets and canals,
only straighter, and that there
the shadow always reigned,
and there was never any wind; he consoled himself with silence
so similar to eternity that between these walls
you might not to be afraid of time. He knew
that he would never get old, that the illnesses
would beat him before life could make him tired,
and that a life devoted to cataloging
was not so bad: and something (the library cards) was growing
but look at the years – they are contrary.
We have only those which are not inscribed
and there are fewer of them
with each spring.
We need to look at life philosophically,
he used to say
reaching for the bread with butter wrapped in paper;
then shook crumbs from the table and
took out a little volume of Pascal.
Something childlike in his soul sighed:
ah, why am I not as clever as he is!
What a blessing it would be for a soul
to soar into the pure empyrean space.
and notice neither dust nor bread with butter.
But the voice fell silent and the eyes kept reading.

When I look at blindness and misery,
at the silent world, at the darkness, where a man
is abandoned, alone, lost
in this corner of the universe and doesn't know
who sent him and why,

nor what will be after his death –
I am terrified as though while sleeping,
I was blown to a desert island
and, upon waking,
didn't know
how I got there
or how to get out.

And the library suddenly ceases to be
a library
and the straight hallways cease to be straight
and the catalogs disintegrate
and the letters become
just hooks and squiggles
and in the midst of it Gnedich (*but is he Gnedich?*)
grasps with one hand for the desk
and with the other for the chair
so he will not fall into the gulf
that from the left is tearing the floorboards,
and then from the right.

Beyond the walls, it feels like Petersburg,
or some other city
where people walk on the streets,
having not yet managed to die.
A blizzard
rises like a slow snake
over the Finnish swamp
and moves toward the capital, gaining strength.
It sings and, within its song there is
as much meaning as in the aria that
the public will listen to in the evening.

He cannot remain at the service.
He grips his fur coat and throws it over his shoulders,
his hands barely obeying him, as if
they belong to someone else;
he descends down the stairs,
steep as a cliff, –
the one who descended to the bottom is already not the same
as the one who began descending. A snowstorm
hits him in the face:
– *This will teach you humility* –
but does he need to be taught? He always knew
that he was a nonentity,
and this nothingness under the weight of the fur coat
moves his feet along the street,
and the blizzard again whips at his cheeks,
and, in tears,
he says: – I am still something!
Moisture and wind blind his eyes, but he feels
the warmth and salinity of his tears,
wanders up to his house, inserts the key
into the keyhole.
He shakes the snow off the heels, and his
poodle Malvina, ears waving, hastens to meet him.
In a hurry he starts a fire to warm him up,
but cannot get warm.
When I look at your blindness and misery,
at the silent world,
at you in darkness,
as though you were brought to a desert island
and were left there....

He gets up and walks around the room
walking, walking, walking, and trying to reassure himself that
he has a body,
that there is furniture around him and wallpaper on the walls,
his glance falls on the bookshelf
and his cheeks flush with shame:
for some reason he still keeps
the fruit of his youth's madness –
the novel "Don Corrado de Guerrera;
or the Spirit of Revenge and Treachery of Spaniards."
He wrote it through long lonely nights
when he was twenty
imagining this would win the hearts of his female readers.
He takes the book with two fingers and
casts it into the garbage.
He thought he was a writer,
but it turned out not to be so.
(We know who we are merely when we are loved,
we are those who are loved, and only that.
Otherwise we are nothing).
He falls into a chair and buries his face in his hands.
Malvina caresses his feet, a cat on a couch
is awakening, stretching his paws
and showing the world his fair belly;
the room is warming up
and Gnedich is sleepy but he forces himself
to get up and go to the desk
where there is a copy of *The Iliad*.
He should light candles,
otherwise he will go blind
(*already a Cyclops*), and pour fresh ink.
A sun then

a sun then touched
the valleys
a sun touched the valley with rays
then again
now the morning sun – *whose rays* –
merely struck the meadows....
climbed into the sky
from the ocean, where waters
roll softly, deeply flowing.
They (*who are they? two armies or
dead Greeks with the living?*)
they met each other,
it was so difficult to recognize the dead,
the living ones loaded them onto carts
washed off the blood, felt
tears roll down
but Priam forbid them
to cry out in grief
and in silence
they put their dead into the fire
and when it had eaten everything, they left
for the sacred city of Troy,
the Achaeans too put their dead in a fire
and when it had eaten everything –
depart
to the empty ships.

He falls asleep and dreams about the empty field.
But in the morning he cannot remember his dream.
He carefully dresses in front of the mirror
and goes to work
where he stays until evening, and in the apartment

Elena enters with a soft smile.
She cleans while he's not there,
cleans the dust from them plaster heads in the study room,
from a clock, and from many books.
Before there were less;
once there was only one sofa, and now there are three,
and the carpet on the floor looks Persian,

The three-foot mirror need be cleaned
so there are no smudges.
Master is reflected in it.
(She almost forgot his face;
before 'twas the porter as let her in,
and now a valet).
But she reckons there are more books,
more candles burned down.
There is a woman on the wall dressed like a savage –
maybe she is an outlandish queen.

Elena kneels
to pull out the paper basket from the desk,
and there she finds a small book in the trash
and another one.
What can she do? Carry them to the garbage?
What if he looks for 'em?
But if she leaves 'em,
they 'ull say she worked badly.
So she hides the books at her bosom
If they ask her, she will bring 'em,
if not, she'll throw 'em out later herself.
Elena shakes up a bed in his bedroom.

Do the gentries
have noble dreams?
Or do they dream the same filth as everyone else?
Coming back home at night, she hopes to
have some noble dream,
sumthin' like princess from that pic'ter
or dances as that agoin'on
in them stone manors.
For at the river-sides are such low banks
and beggars a-sittin' at the bridges,
danglin' their stumps,
main thing to not look at them for long
so they won't spook ye at night.

SONG VIII

"Gnedich, tell me, why did I hide
 in dreams as a child? –
 Batyushkov wrote. –
"Probably so that I wouldn't grieve for my mother,
 yet think about her in a different way,
 as though neither madness nor death existed,
 but solely one moment, taken from my memory's depths,
 when she was with me,
 and that moment went on in my dreams.

I created an Italy for myself,
beautiful as a mother,
so that she would embrace me in her arms.
But even here it is lonely.

We left for Baia in the evening,
to see the ruins through the water of the Gulf at dawn.
Do you know about this city? Of course you do, you know
everything.
It is a port city near the Stygian marshes,
here Pliny looked on as the volcano spewed the flames
that killed Pompeii.
Being Roman, he was accustomed to the sight

and knew that at death one ought to look on calmly,
(even at his own) and yet he was horrified.
In this port Caligula built a bridge of many boats,
and his horse, placing his hooves
stepped from boat to boat until he came to Puteoli, –
so thus a madman outwitted an astrologer,
who told him:
"Ride a horse over the bay,
and you'll become an emperor."
Here Nero twice tried to kill his mother,
and in the end he succeeded;
he played the harp to forget himself.

We went into a semicircular temple of Echo,
half-filled with water,
clapped our hands and then heard
invisible hands applaud for us
as though on command.
I felt like a gladiator in the arena,
but my slain opponent
was as invisible as the audience.

At dawn, before getting into the boat,
I saw a boy on the beach
throwing flat pebbles into the sea,
so that they would bounce off the water,
and only then sink.
I rummaged around in the nooks of my memory,
hoping to discover myself as a child
in a similar pastime
but found nothing;
I remembered only things I dreamt

as a child and a youth;
I barely touched life-
like these pebbles skimming the sea surface, -–
just a bit.
If only I could
go back and restore
the life I missed while dreaming,
about which I can only wonder.
Monsieur used to take me to a forest
and a birch grove,
but I cannot remember their scents.
There had to be birds singing,
and if I were different,
I would learn to imitate their whistle.
And who were these girls
whom I met sometimes in living rooms
and, blushing with shame, turned away from them,
not getting the chance to glance at their faces,
whether they were pale or, on the contrary, shiny with sweat.
Not one of them was Eleanor,
but unlike her, they *existed*.

I stepped into the boat, afraid to miss
its woodenness and rocking,
I greedily inhaled the smell of the sea,
so that I could tell you: I breathed it!
The real sea, not the one
I saw in my dreams at night,
when the bed was rocking
and calling itself
in the false language of dreams
a boat.

The boatman said: guarda così è bello!
On my right the Spanish castle was pink and golden,
on the left the shadows were still thick,
and empty boats quivered like black grains
in the blue predawn water.
But I could not,
I could not forget myself
and become this bay.
Dreams creep up and rise, like glass
between me and the world.

The sun has risen,
rays penetrated the water's depths
illuminating the underwater streets,
porticoes and colonnades;
the boatman explained with a click of his tongue:
'It was Baia – but then the sea came.'
We hung from the boat
and looked at the motionless city under the sea:
on these streets people once walked,
and the most beautiful women of the empire
rested in the shade of the arcades.
Now only water fills the emptiness of the homes, –
but who would dare to assert that all of this is gone?
After all they were beautiful, these matrons of the past,
and beauty, if you believe Plato, is eternity and truth;
therefore, they still exist,
and in the astrologer's mica dish they distinguish my features,
and laugh at the silly Hyperborean,
that believes in himself, but not in them.

But the sea
says that they don't exist,
that maybe, they never did,
there is only me,
who cannot touch anything –
neither that which was, nor that which is.
Caught in a web of my own dreams,
a stunted poet,
and your obedient servant
with a false name
Batyushkov."

When they brought this letter,
Gnedich was still asleep
and the message waited for him in the living room,
on the table, where dust did not yet have the chance to
accumulate.

...Elena came out of the church
on the feast of St. Mary- Who-Sets-Snow-on-Fire
Soon everything will turn into streams,
frozen rivers will crack
and will move ice floes.
She liked to watch as snow turned into water,
when with the spring's roar everything moves, hastening,
exposing the shameless land even here, in the city.
Her shawl slipped off her shoulders,
the wind played with the colorless hair
that had escaped from her braid.
Mary of Egypt was a harlot
but withdrew to the desert,
and became like a walking corpse

from mortification.
On the icon you cannot even make it out,
if it is man or a woman:
the arms and legs are like sticks,
the face tiny.
Elena jumps over a creek and thinks:
all that separates us
disappears because of holiness,
man and woman are the same,
old and young, servant and master
the dead and the living.

She remembers the one-eyed Gnedich:
he is half-blind and pockmarked, –
but he cannot be like that in truth.
They just gave 'im that face t' wear, like a hat
and angels will remove it on Judgment Day,
and under it will be a handsome gentleman
like from an oleograph,
because as a child he was probably handsome.
She imagines that she takes him,
not disfigured yet by smallpox,
by his hand and jumps over the stream,
as if she were his nanny.

That spring, everybody walked constantly,
the city was restless and swarmed like an anthill:
couriers hurried from one office to another,
burghers visited each other for tea,
and fiddled with lace napkins in their fingers
when there was nothing more to talk about.
It was getting warmer and warmer,

dandelions sprouted near dirty roads,
and many years later one writer did not believe
that in his youth there were still flowers on the streets
and lilacs grew in the gardens,
(later all was covered in stone and immortalized).
He questioned every memory
whether was truth or mere imagination,
and if it passed the exam,
he wrote it down in his memoirs.

In the evening he saw the lighted windows
in the flat on the third floor
when he walked on Sadovayia street.
He did not know who lived there now,
but once, when he was very young,
he, with his friend – an actor, climbed these stairs
to visit Gnedich,
and when Gnedich got ready to read from his translations,
the writer's friend furtively nudged him in the ribs,
and whispered: now he'll howl.
Gnedich indeed started to howl,
to shriek, to cry, to wail
about the deeds of Diomedes and Nestor the Elder.
Malvina the dog hid under the couch in fright
and whined from out there more plaintively than the host,
while Gnedich listed the powerful Achaeans and
brushed a candlestick along with the candle onto the floor.
The guests rushed to pick it up so that the house
                                        wouldn't burn down,
but Gnedich grabbed them by their hands
and pointed his finger at the face of one, then at another,
and screamed:

"this evil dog that darts would not destroy!"
 then he came to his senses, embarrassed, and blushed,
 They asked whether everything was alright,
 he did not want to answer.

But they kept thanking him for a long time
and he cheered up
and made them promise that they would come again.
They laughed on the stairs later
and remembered, while going outside,
this evil dog
this evil dog.

Now the writer cannot find the words
to describe the distance
between those stairs and today's office –
like a stream in the spring it runs somewhere until it dries out,
and he cannot understand if all of it was good
or
it didn't matter.

SONG IX

Behind the window glass,
on the edge of the window sill
a pigeon ruffled its feathers.
Gnedich looked at the bird and at the gray sky.
It's cold, probably.
The two of them,
it was not at all like with a cat or dog, –
pets are like people,
but a pigeon, although an inhabitant of the city, was wild.
As if by mutual agreement, they stood frozen
and spoke wordlessly, thoughtlessly.
The likelihood of such conversation penetrates
the very essence of living beings,
because in one thing, at least, the pigeon and Gnedich were alike:
they were both alive.

This one was much prettier than the usual blue-gray
fat pigeons, –
it was grayish-white
with a streamlined body and a curved beak,
its tail was long;
sometimes the pigeon briskly scratched its feathers,
but then became motionless again,

and only two feathers fluttered in the wind.
The pigeon's body trembled slightly.

But then it rose and started to walk
back and forth along the window sill,
with its head jerking,
and Gnedich felt
that they were utterly different
and had never been the same:
a man with memory and a will,
and a dot-eyed bird
that walks back and forth
and cannot decide: to fly away or not.

But once it departs – what will I feel?
Will I be lonely – for we were the same
(perhaps), and now the bird walks
and is about to fly away.
Or will I feel relieved
that I can step away from the window
and continue the translation,
because the whole time,
while I was watching a pigeon through the glass
my thoughts sought to go back to work.

The pigeon continued to walk, jerking its beak,

and then suddenly again – and it took off
with a full-throated cry
and vanished into the sky.
Gnedich was extraordinarily overjoyed
as though he himself was this pigeon

and it was his cry,
and it was he who just flew away
and vanished.
But who is this gentleman
standing at the window
and eagerly looking at the street?
This is me, I forgot myself
but now I am coming back.

Zephyr and Boreas,
Western and Northern winds,
they blow from Thrace,
descend upon the sea
full of fish,
waves
cast out seaweed
on the white sand.

Translator,
the winds from the North and the West blow upon you,
your thoughts have just flown to Thrace,
but now
waves carry you
like a goddess on a shell
to the shore of a paper sea,
and no one recognizes you.

Nestor the horseman furtively
winks to Odysseus and whispers:
you'll persuade Achilles to return to the battlefield,
after all you are smarter than the others.

They wander along the seashore,
you follow them
leaving the prints of invisible feet
on wet sand.
You'd like to linger,
enter up to your knees into the water,
but you cannot lose them from your sight.

Look: Achilles is playing the lyre;
he destroyed a city, killed all its inhabitants,
and took away only this lyre.
Now he plucks the strings
with the fingers
that held a spear
and sings of heroes' glory –
the glory of the one-eyed Ukrainian
who shivers in the capital city,
who sneezes in the office because of book dust,
and after coming home,
dips a pen in the inkwell
like a spear into the body of the enemy,
and imbues the paper with words.

Achilles glimpses the guests and stops playing.
He calls them and the maids
set a pot on the flaming fire and cut a sheep's throat
and then they all eat
unhurriedly, joyfully –
like Russian landlords who visit each other
for lunch, and eat just as long
and engagingly – but doze afterward
in deep armchairs under buzzing flies...

"The wealth of Troy, the temples of Apollo,
  the treasures of the Achaeans and the Trojans,
  all are ashes compared to life,
  all can be purchased, but if the soul,

  like a zephyr, flies away from the body
  you will not catch it.
  My mother told me:
  should you fight and die for Troy – you'll be forever famous,
  but return home, and you will live long and peacefully,
  in ignominy.
  (And Gnedich recalls
  that later not Achilles himself but Achilles' shadow,
  whilst rising from Hades to Odysseus,
  uttered: "I was right then!
  Oh, better be the last of the last
  among the living
  than to be king among the dead.")

"My friend Batyushkov! I reply:
  if life is like a dream, all within it is easy –
  to write poetry,
  to pierce the enemy with the bayonet,
  to fall in love, to despair,
  even to commit suicide –
  all is possible in a dream, all is reversible,
  but if you suddenly wake up,
  for example, when a bullet hits the skull,
  you realize instantly
  you never lived after all.

A rooster cries frantically
that we should wake up,
and listen to the sounds of the earth,
where the day laborer takes his plow and plows
and does not doubt the fact that he lives,
or that he is going to die.

You say: I do not want to be like him
to obey the natural circle of sweat and ash,
but rather wish to be like the infant Achilles
so Phoenix would sit me down on his lap,
and cut meat into small pieces for me,
and wipe my mouth if it is messy.
We want to be warm
as if we were in a mother's womb,
and have someone sit us on his lap,
and press us against his chest.

But if we were truly born, Batyushkov,
into the cold and loneliness,
at least on our deathbeds
we will not deceive ourselves if we say:
"We lived."

Uncertainty takes hold of him,
and dreams overpower him,
laughing at his attempt at rebellion.
The pen falls from his fingers,
and somewhere far away,
near the Achaeans' camp,
next to the walls
of the long ago destroyed Troy,

out of Greek words
Homer erects a tent
wherein peace and friendship are hidden.
It's late.
Fireflies flicker, cicadas sing,
Achilles and an apple-cheeked slave-girl go to bed,
and Patroclus with the graceful maiden Iphis
falls asleep under the patterned coverlet.
The sleeping heroes have the faces of Gnedich and Batyushkov.

Life, forgive me this departure!
I'll return soon
to your cold.

SONG X

Elena unfolded a towel
and placed books on the desk,
books that she found at Gnedich's
and did not dare to throw away.
Her brother – the lame Ignat,
and Thomas who learned to read and write from the deacon
sat on a bench and watched the burning candle
whose crackling
was warding off the darkness from their faces.
But even though the darkness only huddled in corners
it knew that it would conquer the whole house,
not just the basement and the attic,
and the place where the goblin lived behind the stove,
until he died of starvation
because Elena and her brother
forgot to give him a saucer of milk at night.
(Before his death he vowed to harm them,
but was too weak,
and because he knew that he could neither
curse them nor forgive them,
he became sad,
for evil is merely the absence of goodness, –
and such a non-presence was dying).

Thomas cleared his throat; and with importance, plaintively
 started to read,
Ignat and Elena sat open-mouthed.
At first they imagined
 that they were at church,
but suddenly they were transported to Hispania,
the bloody and terrible land,
far away from their village.

A black shadow covered the fields,
Night came and silence fell.
The silver moon from the clouds
Went out to share my sorrow.
Oh moon, my languorous friend,
Pale queen of night, please come to me!

The river was dammed by dead bodies,
piles of bodies littered the valley,
a wife, swimming in her own blood,
kissed her husband's blue lips,
and a nocturnal bird
howled and
howled.

There once was a man named Juan,
a terrible robber captain,
and he had two sons –
good Alonso and evil Corrado.
He did not love his good son,
but with the evil one he sailed on a ship
and robbed travelers.

Suddenly a storm arose,
waves ascended to the clouds,
and while falling, divided
the water down to the very bottom.
At this moment every human being's heart
was exposed:
those who loved someone rushed to them,
a faithful spirit fell back on its faith,
but the avaricious one looked after his trunks, –
at that moment Corrado
pushed his father Juan
into the sea.
Oh, unseen villainy –
the son rose against his father.

The second evening they were reading:
Juan swam and swam, until he emerged onto the shore.
Thankful to the Lord,
he repented his crimes,
began to live virtuously,
and assisted poor farmers,

but Nature
had became enraged at Juan's son
and crashed the ship,
all the robbers sank;
but a wave
carried Corrado to shore,
he lay there naked on the sand.

O Moon, you find me
Without a friend, but with a gentle soul –

When I remember the pleasant evenings,
I shed a river of tears...

An English lord was walking along the shore.
He glanced at the youth lying on the sand
and asked him, Who are you?
The other answered, I am of noble origin.
The lord loved him like a son,
he gave him clothes and shoes,
and brought him back to the world,
but vicious Corrado
got himself such a friend
named Ree-Chard, with whom he played cards,
gambled, and lost all his money;
then they robbed the lord
and fled abroad!

The third evening they were reading:
when the two evil friends reached Hispania's borders,
one Spaniard, full of perfidy,
began to incite them
to kill his rich uncle,
good old Perlat.
In Spain for seven rubles
you can find such a thug
who would not stop at anything:
one Spaniard had to carry out the assassination,
and for two days he sat in a swamp waiting,
he ate all kind of grass and roots,
on the third day he finally saw the victim
and cut his throat
with a hellish hatred.

Corrado, Ree-Chard and their servant Booth
entered the home of the old man Perlat,
forced him to rewrite his will,
and smothered him with pillows.

You thought you would become happy,
But suddenly a blow – you die,
Like a spring flower you fade!
You are struck with a sharp scythe,
Here you are buried in a grave!

As a reward, Corrado received a Gothic castle –
very big, almost like the Royal one,
amid the mountains and the forests,
with Gothic towers at the corners –
those great barbarian towers –
and under the North tower
there was a great underground cavern.
When Corrado heard
that someplace there was another rich old man,
he rushed to find him,
to kill him and take his money.
He found him and saw
it was his father, Juan!
The son gritted his teeth in fury
and locked him in the dungeon.

The fourth day they were reading:
and yet Corrado had a wife,
gentle Olympia.
He first fell in love,
but afterward it seems he fell out of love.

He sent her to live in the castle,
and he himself went to war somewhere else, –
because he wanted to kill more people.

Where have those moments gone,
When I walked around with my sweetheart,
And under the shade of an oak
Rested at her sweet bosom?

Juan in the cave did not know
about Olympia,
Olympia, upstairs in the rooms, did not know
about Juan,
once she was walking along the river
with her face lowered
and thoughtful,
and listened to the turtledove's
languid and plaintive wailing.

Where have those moments gone,
When the blood flowed faster,
When the heart beat more rapidly,
And tender passion revived us?

And suddenly
a fellow was rushing toward her.
She asked: Who are you?
And he replied: Oh, do not ask!
Oh my dreadful fate!
I am Alonzo, the evil Corrado's brother,
poverty and providence drive me.
The lady then burst into tears,

and he asked her: Ah, why
have you taken the form of a Crocodile?
Only crocodiles shed tears.
Better take the form of a Siren.
who loves to laugh.

(They were not entirely clear
about what the book meant here,
but still they were scared.)

And Alonzo
continued his sad story...
But then he became ill!
Olympia looked after him,
she was terribly curious
as to when he would continue his tale.

The fifth evening they were reading:
Corrado's father
was sitting in his terrible cave.
Nobody came to see him.
a gravedigger named Infante
once casually glanced in the window
and saw: O God! There was an old man!
And the gravedigger burst into tears
because he had a kind heart,
and together with a servant
they helped the old man
escape the dungeon.

When Alonzo recovered,
he, like all Spaniards,

played the guitar.
Olympia listened
and sang along:

When – but ah! – why do sorrows multiply?
Why touch this string?
For what? For what? It will hurt, –
And my poor heart will burst.

Suddenly Corrado runs in
and plunges a knife into Alonzo's chest
with a gleeful yell: Ha!

Fratricide, fratricide!
Olympia cursed him
and fell down utterly lifeless.
Just at this moment Corrado killed
almost all of the others.

But then Corrado had terrible, terrible dreams.
Bloodstained ghosts arose.
He ran through the castle
but could not hide anywhere.
"Oh! What is happening to me!" he repeated, and then fell
down on the nearest sofa.

Time flew away, it's gone.
My joy vanished.
A deep abyss devoured it
And it will never return.

But the avenger of innocent blood
named Don Ribeiro
was already nearby.
He broke into the Gothic castle with his band,
and the old man Juan was with him as well.
The old man told Corrado:
Son, I forgive you!
But Corrado rushed at him like a tiger
and stabbed him!
They began to arrest him –
he did not want to give himself up,
he took his neck and tried to choke himself.
All the same, he was seized and
taken to his execution.
Don Ribeiro turned out to be the son of Infante
the gravedigger.
He married Olympia
and as we say
they lived happily ever after and for good.

When Thomas finished reading,
they sat in silence for a long time.
Tears rolled down their cheeks.
They did not wipe them off.
All kinds of astonishing things happen in the world!
You live and don't know
about them.
It's not like catching a thief at the fair,
or when Mitrofan has done in his own wife while drunk.
Here is something that will take out your heart and soul!
Your whole being will be shaken...

Where did this gentleman learn all these things
depicted in this book?

On a winter evening, while threading yarn
Elena will tell her friend about
a king, who had two sons:
one good, the another evil;
about the princess Olympia
from the far away land of Hispania.
She married the evil one,
who threw her father into a terrible cave
and strangled her mother with pillows.
The younger brother set off on a journey,
he fought with sirens and crocodiles and
got in a storm, where his ship was swept away,
and he was washed ashore.
There a princess with a thoughtful face was walking.
She found him and nursed him back to health.
But the brothers recognized each other:
the older wanted to kill the younger,
as is customary among the Turks,
but the younger brother was stronger,
he won and freed the father from his cave,
with whose blessing
he and the princess
were married.

The friend would listen and nod.

In Gnedich's apartment
Elena knows the location of every little thing,
and which of them have gotten worn out over the years,

so as to throw them away,
and which ones are given away or lost,
because they suddenly disappeared without a trace;
she knows where the paint on the walls has faded,
which were once *a pure blue*,
she brushes dust off the books
of which there are more and more,
and looks at the pages with strange characters.
She sees potted plants wither,
sees them die, how new ones arrive,
sees them die, see new ones arrive,
and when rubbing the parquet, she notices
that it becomes harder to bend down.
She is not a serf, she is free,
by her own will she came for this job
so many years ago that she lost track of them,
and she saw the master only once –
then, at the very beginning.

She does not know whether he is happy or not.
Sometimes there are flowers in the bowl,
sometimes knickknacks appear on the desk,
then all disappears,
and only through the ink marks
and shards of broken glass,
by wrinkles on his handkerchief
she guesses at his life.

But is there anything other than vague signs
given to her, for her to know him?
So, between guessing and faith:
he lives here,

somebody paid a visit to him,
he looked at this plant,
he crumpled this napkin.
Who is he – the one you think about
and don't know, –
is he a man?
is he a master?
is he God?

Someday, she will come,
when she is not yet too old,
to clean his apartment,
and he will be sitting
at his desk, or maybe in the chair.
And then she will suddenly,
without daring to look at his face,
fall down at his feet.

SONG XI

In the summer house
a finger traces
the letters, inscribed by pencil
on the windowsill:
ombra adorata.
Beloved shadow
drew these words before becoming a shadow,
and Gnedich touches with a thin finger
the letter O, the letter M, the letter B and so on.
He looks through the window into the garden,
at flowers with enormous heads
disheveled from the wind;
they swing on long thin stems,
which, according to the laws of physics
should break off under the weight of the petals,
but they don't break.
The entire garden and the whole house
are the same color – the color of shadow.
At another window the same hand wrote:
there is life *beyond the grave.*

Fewer and fewer friends remain –
and more of their ghosts,

with a noose around their necks or in Siberian mines.
After the swift and sad uprising
who else needs Achilles and Hector?
The entire translation is finished – and someone whispers:
your life was a joke, merely a child's game,
you hid in books, so as not to think
about who you are,
and why
you were not loved.

He takes a book from the shelf.
Poor Karamzin died in May.
Emptiness and fatigue left over from a past life.
He reads *The History*, but his eyes close,
letters turn into a blank space,
and now his body is left behind, sleeping on the couch,
while his spirit travels with Karamzin
over the endless plain
(which is called Kimmeria by the sleeping ones
and Russia by those who are awake).
To the North people sleep for six months a year,
to the East vultures guard their gold.

"Are we really in exile?"
Karamzin cheerfully asks.
Arms outstretched, they place their hands
under the white feathers falling from the sky
(the air is full of them).
Near the frozen sea warriors in Scythian helmets
fight each other;
Gnedich knows the rules of a match.
He looks at his companion

but he has turned into Suvorov.
The old man winks
and gallops forward on one foot,
crowing like a rooster.
Gnedich lifts his eyes to the sky
and glimpses an Empress sitting on a cloud.
"Speransky!" – Suvorov yells to her and bows.
"Speransky!" – she replies
and bursts into laughter,
moving her skirts.
(Gnedich thought at first,
that maybe the language here
has only this one word).

But the Empress' laughter became muffled,
the sky became a white blanket of clouds,
and next to him, instead of Suvorov,
was a pale creature,
a woman in a patched sweater.
Gnedich struggled to remember where he had seen her –
at a market or in a servant's room? –
she blinked with colorless eyelashes
and said nothing.
Finally, she turned and walked away, quickly,
with her whole body leaning forward.
Gnedich hurried after her.

Snow crackled under his feet.
God! and he was in thin shoes.
The woman's feet were wrapped in rags,
her hands were red from the cold.
He wanted to ask: Where are we?

but only air escaped from his mouth.
They passed through winter and spring, and emerged
in low-growing fir trees.
They walked on the ground covered with moss,
where poisonous berries were hiding.
The woman stopped under a tree
and nodded to Gnedich.

He walked over and saw
his friend, tied to the trunk,
naked – at the mercy of clouds of mosquitoes,
which bit into his body.

Gnedich rushed to him to untie the ropes,
but his fingers stuck to the resin, and the knot did not give in.
Batyushkov's lips moved,
and Gnedich bent down to his lips,
expecting to hear a single word –
Speransky –
which was probably a password there;
but quietly, like the rustling of the wind in the trees,
Batyushkov whispered: *lasciate,*
lasciate.

Gnedich woke up with a start,
he held his head in his hands
and started to rock back and forth.
Oh, my friend, even in that nightmare
you did not forget Italian.
Lasciate – leave, –
but what?
We left you in a German asylum,

although we were told that there was no hope,
now not a day goes by that we do not feel guilty.
How are you doing there, my friend,
beloved shadow?

Behold, the angels of the castle, standing on a hill, covered with
trees, and below the hill a village on the river bank,
and many boats at the dock.

Behold, the angels of the towers and bastions and the
surrounding fortification wall, and angels of the garden with
a variety of flowers and herbs.
Behold, the demons of those who walk through the clinic's
garden, each of them says within his heart: there is no God.
Demon-doctors are watching them from the pathways,
scattered with small stones, physician, heal thyself.
Angels of the room placed a desk and a bed in there, but left
the walls bare and the corners empty.
The angel Eternità soars in the emptiness of this room, he covers
his face with two wings, with two others he covers his legs, and
on two wings he flies from one wall to another, and in circles
above my head, like a mosquito.
The angel of wax is at first hot, then cold, and if you are neither
cold nor hot, but lukewarm, I will spit thee out of my mouth;
he is malleable under my fingers, assumes one shape, then
another, but then returns to a lack of form.
My teardrop can burn a hole in the table, dissolve the wall,
pierce the shell of the world, but like any God, I'm hiding
and trying not to cry.
In the morning the Archangel Michael brings breakfast
with one flap of his wings.

At noon the Archangel Gabriel brings lunch
                              with two flaps of his wings.
But the Angel of Sickness flaps his wings eight times like
                              a swan trying to take flight.
In Mainz in the year 1096 Satan took a martyr's death.
Konstantin Batyushkov has a letter from Christ, which certifies
that he, Konstantin, is God, so his nails and hair
                              can drive away demons.
But at night the demons climb on the ceiling and fill the room
with a horrible stench. They whisper spells all night, to incite
him to lustful acts with his right hand, but he covers his ears
with his palms.
The first demon has his father's face, the second the face of his
mother, and the third one the face of his sister, –
                              then he shuts his eyes.
But in the morning, the brother-Sun rises up and drives the
enemies away and Batyushkov shouts after them:
Why do you chase me? Why do you slander me?
Have I really offended anyone with my poems?
Have I, in fact, hurt someone?
You persecuted me and mixed poison in my drink and food; you
extinguished stars with the saliva on your fingers;
                              and you sent people to follow me.

I tried to cut my throat, but you did not let me.
I tried to burn books, but you printed new ones.
I taught a cat to write poems, and already they've turned
                              out to be not that bad.
I wrote to Byron: Milord, send me a teacher of English, so that I
may read your writings in the original! And pray to my bride.

Angel Innocence – Hallelujah – Christ is Risen – non sum
dignus – Kyrie Eleison – Ave Maria!

My bride says: you'll always remain in this castle, the castle
named Sonnenstein, which means Sunstone, in Saxony on Elbe.

Until other angels come, cold-eyed angels in leather coats, angels
made half of snow and half of fire.

They will take out the possessed from the hospital wards and will
line them up on the grass and the flowers of a garden, which is
surrounded by a fortress wall.
And shoot them, and dig pits to bury them.
And the possessed will understand, dying,
                                        that they were angels, too,
but used to dwell in a prison of flesh,
and now the whistling bullets have freed them from their bodies.

And they will thank their saviors and sing out
                                        from under the ground:
Holy, Holy, Holy Lord of Sabaoth,
heaven and earth are full of Thy Glory.

SONG XII

The landlord Olenin's grandchildren
mingled with the servants' kids
playing tag. The morning sun was not hot.
They ran barefoot on the grass and yelled: Eeeh! and Aaah!
Beyond the meadow was a river, and a grove behind it,
but they only saw
each other's fleeing backs.
one had to overtake the other, to catch him
then turn around, and run away.

Fedya Olenin stopped momentarily
and put his hand to his forehead, shielding himself from the sun,
so as to examine a man
who was sitting on the hill, and looking
not at them, but somewhere in the sky –
at clouds, probably.
He recognized Gnedich, his parents' guest,
by his long legs and arms,
and yelled to him:
"Nikolai Ivanovich, come here!"
Gnedich shook his head, but Fedya
continued to wave invitingly, more as a joke.

Then suddenly the tall, slouching man got up
and ran to the children
(even here he, like a city dandy,
was dressed immaculately).
They scattered in all directions
trying to dodge him,
and he playfully raced after them and laughed.
Until he choked up with a cough.
Then everyone stopped, but he began to run again
and let the smallest girl catch him,
and later he again chased after Fedya, and his sister Sonya,
and Akulina, the laundress's daughter,
and Vasya, the shoemaker's son.
Then Fedya shouted: "Break!" –
all obeyed him and
threw themselves down on the grass, breathing loudly.
Gnedich sat down, carefully tucking his legs under him,
and wiped the sweat from his forehead.

"So Nikolai Ivanovich," – Fedya asked him, –
"Tell us
about the Trojan war and about Elena!"
Everything was pleasant on this summer day –
whether running or listening.
Gnedich cleared his throat and began
in a solemn voice:
"At the feast of the gods, they forgot to invite Eris, the goddess of
discord,
and then she craftily planted an apple
labeled: to the most beautiful..."

Akulina was sitting in front of Fedya,
a scarf slipped over her shoulders.
He saw her disheveled hair,
her freckled cheek.
She stretched with her whole body toward a flower
and broke the stem,
to weave it into a wreath, heavy and lush,
which would wither tomorrow.
The smell of her sweat mixed with
the smell of clover and lungwort.
How did Greece smell – surely not also of clover
and dandelions?
Or was it a salty sea smell, when the wind blew?
Fedya chewed a stalk of grass,
if he stretched out his arm, he would touch Akulina,
she would drop the wreath out of surprise,
and would turn,
and would show the gap
between her front teeth in a smile.
Fedya jumped up and shouted: "Let's play again!" –
All responded with cheerful laughter,
and started to run again,
he sprang from the ground
like a young deer,
and did not let anyone catch up to him.

Then they heard the bell calling them to lunch,
the children of the manor went in one direction,
the peasants' children in another,
and all had a long lunch, as was customary on the estate,
and then they rested.

In the afternoon Gnedich reclined in the guest room
and felt a pain in his bones,
that nobody believed.
Friends dismissed it –
they said: you're still young, forty is not seventy.
He takes out a notebook and carefully inscribes the title:
"The story of my illness.
From my childhood I used to feel pain
in my stomach and knees; I had measles, smallpox, worms,
I ate a lot of meat and tempting food, suffered
                                        from stomachaches,
in the fall and spring I felt an overall weariness
in strength, a melancholy and sadness.
One spring morning, when I was drinking my coffee
                                        and smoking a pipe,
I noticed a small amount of blood
in the phlegm from my chest.
The blood did not appear again, but a cold
always struck my throat and caused a cough,
because for many years I strained my throat,
while rehearsing roles
with the tragic actress Semyonova,
and so I grew gradually hoarse.
And my hands and feet, over many years
felt either cold, or burning hot
several times a day.
The pain in the throat particularly intensified at night
or when I went outside,
so that often I could neither sleep nor move.
Finally a doctor examined my throat and announced
that he found *ulcera syphilitica* –

this shocked me; I called another doctor;
they both stood over me,
then withdrew to another room,
and when they returned, they pronounced that there is
definitely *ulcera syphilitica* in my throat,
and accordingly..."

He pulls his pen from the paper and thinks about the child,
he once was – before the smallpox, the measles, the rubella,
before he lost an eye, before
his body grew up and became awkward,
before his throat was covered with sores:
the child who sat on his mother's lap,
the smooth child, kissed and hugged,
carried from room to room and cradled,
and Gnedich wants to believe that this love,
                                which he does not remember,
was a prediction of another love,
and of a different existence.

Dipping his pen into the inkwell,
he wrote with tears of resentment:
"Due to many reasons, maybe unfair ones,
I do not agree with their opinion,
nor with their treatment."

Fedya was dozing in a chair,
and woke up when they called him for dinner.
He tried to remember his dream:
as though he had sent a request somewhere,
and the answer had apparently come back positive
(but he did not remember either a question or an answer).

After dinner he went up to his room,
lit some candles and took a sheet of paper.
He liked to draw horses, guards,
guns, tents, bridges and rivers,
crossed by guards on horses,
and sometimes he stayed up after midnight to draw,
but this evening the pencil did not obey his hand,
the lines came out crooked and the horses
did not look like horses, but more like dogs,
and when he got lost in his thoughts, the pen
took to sketching
the shape of a girl's body .

He stood up, walked to the window and pressed his forehead
against the cold glass – it always helped.
Outside somebody had left a broom, in the twilight a chicken
was moving around a woodpile behind the shed,
for some reason he wanted to remember all of this – forever,
as though later there would be no chicken and no shed.
And he saw, in the darkness, a white shirt,
Akulina walked across the yard – she raised her head.
He did not have time to hide,
their eyes met, and there was something forbidden
in this glance.

He made a gesture with his hand: *wait for me*.
She lowered her head and it was as though she was drawing
something
on the ground with her bare foot – he could not see what.
Fedya blew out the candle,
pressed his fingers to his temples, and then
rushed down the stairs.

A NOTE ON THE TRANSLATOR

Elena Dimov is a translator of Russian. She was born in Vladivostok, Russia and holds a M.S. in Oriental Studies from Far Eastern University and a Ph.D. in History from the Russian Academy of Sciences. She has lived in Moscow, Hamburg, and Sofia. Since 1999, she has been living in Charlottesville, Virginia, where she works at the University of Virginia and teaches a class in Russian Language and Culture. She edits the UVA website Contemporary Russian Literature at UVA. She is currently studying Russian bard poetry as well as translating Russian literature into English, including works by Joseph Brodsky and Maria Rybakova.

Dear Reader,

Thank you for purchasing this book.

We at Glagoslav Publications are glad to welcome you, and hope that you find our books a source of knowledge and inspiration.

We want to show the beauty and depth of the Slavic region to everyone looking to expand their horizons and learn something new about different cultures, different people, and we believe that with this book we have managed to do just that.

Now that you've got to know us, we want to get to know you.
We value communication with our readers and want to hear from you!

We offer several options:

-   Join our Book Club on Goodreads, Library Thing and Shelfari, and receive special offers and information about our giveaways;

-   Share your opinion about our books on Amazon, Barnes & Noble, Waterstones and other bookstores;

-   Join us on Facebook and Twitter for updates on our publications and news about our authors;

-   Visit our site www.glagoslav.com to check out our Catalogue and subscribe to our Newsletter.

Glagoslav Publications is getting ready to release a new collection and planning some interesting surprises — stay with us to find out!

Glagoslav Publications
Office 36, 88-90 Hatton Garden
EC1N 8PN London, UK
Tel: + 44 (0) 20 32 86 99 82
Email: contact@glagoslav.com

Glagoslav Publications Catalogue

- *The Time of Women* by Elena Chizhova
- *Sin* by Zakhar Prilepin
- *Hardly Ever Otherwise* by Maria Matios
- *The Lost Button* by Irene Rozdobudko
- *Khatyn* by Ales Adamovich
- *Christened with Crosses* by Eduard Kochergin
- *The Vital Needs of the Dead* by Igor Sakhnovsky
- *A Poet and Bin Laden* by Hamid Ismailov
- *Kobzar* by Taras Shevchenko
- *White Shanghai* by Elvira Baryakina
- *The Stone Bridge* by Alexander Terekhov
- *King Stakh's Wild Hunt* by Uladzimir Karatkevich
- *Depeche Mode* by Serhii Zhadan
- *Saraband Sarah's Band* by Larysa Denysenko
- *Herstories*, An Anthology of New Ukrainian Women Prose Writers
- *The Hawks of Peace* by Dmitry Rogozin by Leonid Andreev
- *The Battle of the Sexes Russian Style* by Nadezhda Ptushkina
- *A Book Without Photographs* by Sergey Shargunov
- *Sankya* by Zakhar Prilepin
- *Wolf Messing – The True Story of Russia's Greatest Psychic* by Tatiana Lungin
- *Good Stalin* by Victor Erofeyev
- *Solar Plexus* by Rustam Ibragimbekov
- *Don't Call me a Victim!* by Dina Yafasova
- *A History of Belarus* by Lubov Bazan
- *Children's Fashion of the Russian Empire* by Alexander Vasiliev
- *Empire of Corruption – The Russian National Pastime* by Vladimir Soloviev
- *Heroes of the 90s – People and Money. The Modern History of Russian Capitalism*
- *Boris Yeltsin – The Decade that Shook the World* by Boris Minaev
- *A Man Of Change – A study of the political life of Boris Yeltsin*
- *Marina Tsvetaeva – The Essential Poetry*

More coming soon...

www.ingramcontent.com/pod-product-compliance
Lightning Source LLC
Chambersburg PA
CBHW050153110726
47898CB00008B/2783